W9-AEL-442

Kill My Mother

Kill My Mother

A Graphic Novel

Jules Feiffer

Liveright Publishing Corporation
A Division of W. W. Norton & Company
New York London

Printed in the United States of America
First Edition

For information about permission to reproduce selections from this book,
write to Permissions, Liveright Publishing Corporation,
a division of W. W. Norton & Company, Inc.
500 Fifth Avenue, New York, NY 10110

For information about special discounts for bulk purchases, please contact
W. W. Norton Special Sales at specialsales@wwnorton.com or 800-233-4830

Manufacturing by RR Donnelley, Willard OH
Production managers: Anna Oler and Joe Lops

Library of Congress Cataloging-in-Publication Data

Feiffer, Jules.
Kill My Mother : a graphic novel / Jules Feiffer. — First edition.
pages cm
ISBN 978-0-87140-314-8 (hardcover)
1. Noir fiction. 2. Graphic novels. I. Title.
PN6727.F4K55 2014
741.5'973—dc23
2014005844

Liveright Publishing Corporation
500 Fifth Avenue, New York, N.Y. 10110
www.wwnorton.com

W. W. Norton & Company Ltd.
Castle House, 75/76 Wells Street, London W1T 3QT

2 3 4 5 6 7 8 9 0

To Milton Caniff
Will Eisner
Hammett and Chandler and Cain –
John Huston
Billy Wilder
Howard Hawks
And Joan Z. Holden!

Kill My Mother

Part One:

Bay City Blues
1933

Chapter One: Little Annie Hannigan
And now for your listening pleasure-
Miss Ginger Rogers sings her new hit from her new musical, "The Gold Diggers." Sing, Ginger!
Annie, your mother's gonna kill us if she finds us.
Shut up, Artie, and just try to keep up!
We're out of money,
No money honey,
Grin at the bad news,
Just laugh it away!

I could kill my mother.
Sometimes I think I was kidnapped at birth-
And that she's not my real mother.
Except then my father would have had to arrest her. It would have been his duty.
Shut up, Artie.
Annie, you shouldn't talk about your mother that way.
Because he was a cop. Maybe I'll grow up to be a detective like my father, and I'll arrest her.
The only honest cop in the history of prohibition, so they killed him. And what does she do?
She leaves me flat.
To go to work in an office.
I could kill her.
Anyhow, she's not my mother.
Besides, who wants her around the house all day telling me all the things I do wrong.

As if she really cares, or she wouldn't be working downtown for some idiot of a private detective.

But, Annie-

As if she thinks he's gonna actually track down the gang who dumped my father in the river.

But, Annie-

ELSIE!

Will you ever shut up?

Even though I'm taking my first typing class, I bet **I'm** a better secretary than her.

Chapter Two: Elsie at the Office

Elsie, in here now, goddamn it!
What the hell is the matter with you? Have you goddamn gone shopping?
PRIVATE

Didn't I ask you yester-day to type up my report to... to...
Shit! What the hell is the name of my client?
Duane Murdock.
Who gives a crap?
The file! The file! Where's the file?
You were dead drunk.
What you dictated was some gibberish about a girl named Trixie. I took the notes and wrote up the report myself.
It's in front of you. It's hard to see underneath the bourbon bottles.
I don't remember dictating any of this.
You wrote about me and Trixie?
Who the hell do you think you are?
You're fired!
You had passed out cold, and Murdock was screaming for the report. I wrote up the information you dug up-
And sent it over to him. He called a half hour ago to say he was so pleased, he was adding an extra fifty to your fee.
I don't need a goddamned receptionist writing up my-
Fifty bucks?

Are you claiming I didn't dictate this?
You were dead to the world. Head on the desk
Out.
It sounds just like me. Goddamn it, Elsie, I don't impress easy, but-
It was fun. I enjoyed writing it.
You are cute.
Real cute.
I love it when you sound like a detective out of the pulps.
Yeah?
Say, I keep a hotel room across the street.
The Hotel Floozie. I pay the bill.
Funny girl. It's the Hotel Flora.
How about it?
You proved you got brains. I need to see what else you got.
Neil-
I'm late to pick up Annie.
What's an Annie?
My daughter. You've met her.
You have a kid named Annie?
I should know this about the people who work for me.
You're drunk!

I remember! Your kid! Annie! She's mad at you all the time!
She'll get over it.
When you've been around as long as I have, Kiddo, you'll know: No one gets over anything.
Go to hell!
SLAM
Cute. A real addition to the office.
Chapter Three: The Tattoo Artist
Neil Hammond!
You could eat him for breakfast, he's so sexy.
His eyes don't blink.
The way he smokes.
The wisecracks.
The way he drinks.
The whole year my mother's worked for him, I don't think he solved a single case.
I have a crush on Neil Hammond.
You shouldn't be talking to me like this.
Shut up, Artie.
Annie-
I'm talking to your back, it's like you're not even here.
I'm too young for him right now, Neil Hammond-
A fifteen year old without tits-
if she gets him to marry her, my mother, all of us living under the same roof-
Two, three years from now- the way I'll look-
I will take Neil Hammond away from my mother.
You know what that's gonna do to her?
It will kill her.
Hooray.

Chapter Four: The Big Blonde

CLICK
CLICK
CLICK
CLICK
CLICK
CLICK
CLICK
Neil Hammond
CONFIDENTIAL
INVESTIGATIONS
Hello!
Hello!

I'm looking for Neil Hammond, the detective.
You are beautiful.
You are classy.
Close the door
on your way out.
You are out of my league, lady.
I'm searching for...
...this woman.

She disappeared two years ago.
She looks like you.
We are not related.
Not related?
She was my high school drama teacher. Possibly because of the resemblance, we became close. The last time I saw her, she told me she'd been offered a small part in a Boris Karloff horror movie.
After not hearing from her for some months, I made inquiries. There was no Boris Karloff movie.
She has vanished without a trace.
And you want me to find her. Why? If there's no relation...
I have gone from city to city within a hundred-mile radius...
In each city I have hired detectives to find her. No one has come up with anything.
You must have a lot of money to throw around.
I am married to a man who indulges me.
I bet you're used to men indulging you.
You're presumptuous.
That bother you?
Not at all-
Rudeness is often taken for candor these days.

Will $200 do as a retainer?
You will want my name and contact information.
Forget it.
Don't mistake my candor for rudeness, but I don't believe your story.
So I'm not gonna be convinced by any name you give me.
If your so-called teacher is here in Bay City, I'll find her.
Come back in a week.
Would it help to know her name?
Her name is Patricia Hughes.
How tall is she?
Tall. six foot two.
You're pretty tall too. You sure there's no relation?
I'll be back in a week. Do you have a receptionist? The name I will give your receptionist is Normandie Drake.
Doozy of a name. I sure hope it's yours.
One can only hope.

Chapter Five: Elsie, Elsewhere
STORE TO LET
ECONOMY CLEANERS
STORE TO LET
SALE
EVERYTHING MUST GO

Annie!

Got bored waiting went to Library to study
Library...
study...
I just bet!

Chapter Six: Shopping Spree

Here.
What am I supposed to do with this?
It goes in your pocket, stupid!
Also this.
I'm not gonna-
Annie, you're gonna get us both arrested!
For what, for heaven's sake?
Shoplifting! It's against the law!
You're gonna get us into so much trouble!
Think about it, Artie- who'd you'd rather be in trouble with? The store?
Or me?
10% SALE
You are such a fairy!
Don't you call me that!
Take it back, Annie! You take that back!
Let's get out of here before your whining gets us caught.

Chapter Seven: The Come-On

Back already?
No kid?
Not talking?
Fine.
But don't cry, OK?
So what's the story on... Annie?
Never mind.
See why I never married?
Settled down?
Had a family?
You don't mind if we get back to business... I want you to place an ad in both Bay City papers. "Wanted for feature part in new film. Tall blonde, six feet tall or over. Age, late twenties. Casting call, Tuesday through Thursday, 10 AM to 2 PM"
You place the ad, then you rent one of the vacant offices on this floor, a weeks rental. You rent a desk, a couple of chairs, maybe a file or two, a prop phone. Have a sign painted on the door: "Starstruck Productions, George E. Goldwyn, President."
Tuesday through Thursday, that's gonna be your own personal office.
You're gonna see a parade of big, over-the-hill broads who still think they can be movie stars. They'll be lined up and down the hall, for all I know, down the stairs, and around the block. The one we're interested in-

-is the dame in this picture. If she shows up-

-and my guess is she will show up, if she's anywhere in the Bay City area-
She knows we're looking for her, or not?

Your guess is as good as mine. We have a client who, my bet is, she's lying through her teeth.
So we don't have much to go on.

You study the picture, and if we get lucky, she shows up. Say she looks different, say her hair is a different color, say she looks older, say younger, say she's got buck teeth and wears a beard-

-you'll still be able to recognize her. The minute she shows up, you get rid of the others. You run down the hall and get me. I'll be here. Drinking my lunch. Any hour, I'm here, you'll find me. Drinking my lunch.
Kiddo, you think you're up for this job?

Your guess is as good as mine.

Chapter Eight: On the Run

Come back, you!
He's gaining on us, Annie!
He weighs a ton, how could be gaining on us?
We're going to jail!
I'm not gonna let you go to jail.
That's what you say-
But I'm the first person you'd let go to jail.
YOU DON'T STAND A CHANCE, YOU LITTLE THEIVES!
I'm running out of breath, Annie!
Keep running, Artie, or I swear I'll kill you!
I got a stitch in my side!

This should stop him!
When Fatso stops to pick it up, we'll get away!
STOP!
How could he not stop for a fifteen-dollar sweater?
Artie, you throw some-thing!
Like what?
You expect me to think of everything?
This gold watch?
A watch is good.
This rawhide leather wallet?
For God sakes, Artie, throw **something!**
I think he'd definitely stop to pick up the watch-
But I want to keep it!
And I don't care that much about the wallet, but I don't think it will stop him.
The watch would stop him, but I always wanted a Longine Wittnauer, and I hate to lose it!

Chapter Nine: Gotcha!

Don't leave me, Annie!
My name isn't Annie!
Kick him in the balls, Artie!
Tell him your father's best friends with the sheriff!
Lemme go, here's the wallet! I give it to you!
You got nowhere to go, girlie! You're finished.
I'm going to make you pay for this little footrace!
I want my mother!

You're hurting me,
I want my watch
back.
Perfect!
Just the way
I like my women.
Lemme go, you bully! You're
breaking my arm!
POW!
POW!
Please
stop!
THUD!

Chapter Ten: The Invite

You're not listening, Sheila. It's Eddie, The Dancing Master, Longo, top contender for the welterweight crown! You know how hard it was for me to score these ducats?
And now, two hours before fight time, you're backing out because your mother fell down the stairs?
Don't think I don't feel for the old lady, Sheila. I wish her the very best. But you and me had plans, and this is the hottest ticket in-
Sheila? Sheila!
ELSIE!
You are one lucky lady. I got tickets for the big fight tonight.
Is this an invitation?
Neil, I have to be home for Annie.
Anyhow, I don't like fights.
Kiddo, only broads who don't work for me turn down my invites. You go with me to the Bay City Hippodrome tonight, or tomorrow, you go on unemployment. Get your goddamn coat!

Chapter Eleven: The Risk Factor

I only took this job because you promised to help me solve Sam's murder.
But in almost two years you've done absolutely nothing to find my husband's killer.
I liked Sam, but Sam's problem was he was the wrong kind of honest.
For a cop there are two kinds of honest: smart-honest and idiot-honest. Putting your nose where you shouldn't and telling your superiors about it, that's idiot-honest.
There's a serious risk factor involved. For me to say anything more about it would mean I'm being idiot-honest, and I assume the same risk factor Sam did.
Me, I'm smart-honest. I navigate around the risk factors.
But not your Sam.
Which is why I drink this bourbon with you, and he don't.

Excuse me, pal. I come in here on a rainy night for a quiet drink. And you are talking way, way too loud.
So let me see if I get this straight. You would like me to quiet down?
Exactly, pal.
I don't recommend you try my patience, pally.
And your quiet drink! Is this too loud?
Buddy, The last thing I want to do is disturb you-
I have great respect for you and your quiet drink, and your patience.
Am I still too loud?
Is this really the way you want it, pal?
Thanks for asking. No, this is the way I want it.

I notice you've got a gun in your hand.
Seems to be the case.
What if I took that gun away from you and shoved it down your throat?
That would solve the problem of me talking too loud, wouldn't it?
Want it?
Take it.
What...?

Tsk
Tsk
Time's up.
Bad move to spend all that valuable time...
...thinking.
My guess is that they're probably gonna want us to leave about right now.

You enjoyed yourself back there.
Oh?
Think so?
Didn't you?
Let you in on a little secret. Every now and then —
I get this urge- call it a weakness- for a little fun.
Neil, that man was twice your size!
An empty suit.
What about all that talk of yours about a risk factor?
See this here picture?
You either come up with the tall number in this picture or ya start worrying about your own risk factor.

Chapter Twelve: The Tall Woman

That's my father. He was a cop. He died.
That's me and my mother when I was a baby. She looks prettier there than she really is.
Are you hungry? If my mother was here, she could make you something, but she has a job and never comes home.
Come on with me to the kitchen. I don't know what we have to eat. Anything you want you can have. Do you like chicken?
I don't know if we have any. You can leave your bat anywhere. No one will take it.
I found these lamb chops. They're leftovers but I think they're still good. You saved my life. I wouldn't give you anything bad to eat. Want me to hold your bat?
I know you don't talk, but you understand me, right?
Are you nuts? What are you doing?

She's bigger than my father.
She's bigger than YOUR father.
No, she's not.
But that's an idea.
My mother never gave any of my father's clothes away.
They'd fit her great!
Annie! Your mother will kill you!
Anyway, she's filthy.
So we give her a bath.
Next, we have to find her a place to sleep.
You're gonna let her sleep in your house?
We can't let her go back in an alley to live.
But she's not normal!
She can't even talk!
I'll give you ten seconds to shut up, Artie. So how do you think she'll look in this?

Chapter Thirteen: The Dancing Master

I can't believe I found a parking spot.
Neil, you're drunk. It's a risk to life and limb to be in a car with you.
Jeez, you're a lousy date!
I am not your-
Well, well, well-
If it ain't Neil Hammond, half-ass detective.
You come to the fight to make good on the fifty smackers you owe me?
You look like a mess, Gaffney. Go three rounds with a crippled newsie?
Fell outa bed. I coulda worked you in ringside if I knew you was coming. I'm pulling bodyguard for The Dancing Master.
Gonna introduce me to your lady friend?
Mrs. Hannigan, meet Tiny Tim Gaffney, retired bootlegger, pretending to go straight as a private eye.
You don't look so tiny, Mr. Gaffney.
It's a gag, honey bun. I'm the opposite of tiny in ev-ery way. Get my drift?

I don't think I like your friend.
Gaffney?
He ain't no friend of mine.
Here he comes! The next champ!
Why is he called The Dancing Master?
You gotta see him to believe him.
Ladies and gentlemen, may I have your attention, please!
In this corner, tipping the scales at 140 pounds-
Elmo "The Rock" Stavitsky!

And in this corner, tipping the scale at 135 pounds,
Eddie, The Dancing Master, Longo.
That Stavitsky is twice his size.
But it don't mean a thing.
There's the bell, and out dances Eddie Longo.
He's not so much walking as floating.
Stavitsky doesn't look impressed. He moves in on Longo. The Longshoreman vs the Dancer.
Stavitsky misses a roundhouse right, Longo counters with two, three wicked right jabs.

Stavitsky misses a left cross.

Longo dances away. Stavitsky charges.

Longo is not that hard a puncher, but he he nails Stavitsky again. And again.

Bee stings. But those bee stings add up to points. The crowd loves it.

Stavitsky looks confused.

Longo is on him like a matador with a bull.

Stavitsky doesn't know which direction to look. Or who to hit. He could be in the ring with five guys coming from five different directions. The Dancing Master, putting on an impressive show.

Stavitsky doesn't know where he is. Will you look at the big grin on Longo's face! He's laughing at Stavitsky!

Longo on his toes, weaving in and out . . . A right cross staggers Stavitsky. His right eye is closed . . . not that much fight left in him. It's the Dancing Master's party, and he seems to be enjoying it thoroughly.
The nerve of the guy! Can you believe this? He's waving to the crowd! He's calling out to a blonde at ringside.
He's blowing her kisses. I got to admit, she's gorgeous.
LOOK OUT! Stavitsky caught the Dancing Master looking the wrong way!
He's going down!

It's over! The fight is over! The Dancing Master is out like a light.
And his legs are still dancing!
Look at im twitch. This is the first loss for Eddie Longo. Word's out that he's got offers from Hollywood.
He may be in the movies faster than he thinks.
That blonde is following him up the aisle. She is a dish all right.
Whadaya Know!
Will wonders never cease.
My client is the girlfriend of The Dancing Master.

Chapter Fourteen: Vacancy

This way. OK?
There are three empty apartments on this floor.
One of them has to be unlocked.
Not this one.
Maybe this. The lock looks broken.
I Knew it!
I am soooo smart!
Tonight you sleep on the floor. OK? Tomorrow I'll go shopping. I'll bring back a pillow and a blanket. A bed is too big to get out of the store without them noticing.
You can't do this, Annie.

You nearly got us thrown in jail tonight!
Shut up, Artie! The whole reason we're not in jail is her. so stop complaining!
Yeah? And what if your mother finds out? Which she's gonna!
I think she should be OK here until I figure out what to do with her.
We're going now. Are you gonna be OK? I promise to figure out something better. OK?
You're wasting your breath, she doesn't understand a word you're saying.
We are in so much trouble, Annie!
How many times do I have to say it?
Shut up, Artie.

Chapter Fifteen: Stakeout

We stick it out here till we see what they're up to.
Whatever little game she thinks she's playing-
-take it from Neil, I got a trick or two up my sleeve.

We're gonna be here for a while, and I'm out of bourbon.
Don't you think you've had enough?
We passed a liquor store a quarter mile back. Get me a fifth of Cain's bourbon.
You're already drunk.
I'll need money.
I'm good for it.
No, you're not.
I shoulda fired you a long time ago. Here's a sawbuck.
Don't be afraid of the dark.
Ain't been a crime in this neighborhood in five years.

Hey!
What do we have here?
How ya doin', baby?
Come on back!
We got somethin' t'show ya!
Just tryin' t'be friendly!
She's real cute.
For an old lady.
I think I'm in love.
Don'cha worry, honey bun!
We'll walk ya back home!
So you'll be safe.
WINES
LIQUORS

Those three men out there-
They're after me!
Call the police!
... Hello?
Mr., there are three hoodlums outside who can break in here any minute . . .
Did you come in to buy something, or to make trouble?
You are no more safe than I am!
You're an ignoramus. Nobody is safe under capitalism.
The police, who in your hysteria, you wish to summon are the true danger, not those useless bums who, in a socialist state, would have a function to fulfill.
And for you, my phone is out of order.
WINES
Dear God, what's to become of me?
I called for a cop, and they sent me a communist.

Hey, bashful lady, we're gettin' tired o' waitin', you comin' out or are we comin' in?
You hear them? What do you intend to do?
Empty threats from lumpen riff-raff.
But- until the inevitable victory of the Masses, I borrow a tactic from brutish capitalism to protect my property.
Ironic? No argument.
I'll call the police!
You? Call the police? Ironic- no argument.
I'll want a fifth of Cain's bourbon when I come back.
That's my gun! Give back my gun!

Ready for us to walk you home, little lady?
So we get to know you better?
And have a little- you know- fun?
Hey!
C'mon!
My late husband was a police officer. He said I was a better shot than he was.
You kidding me?
You don't know how to use that thing.
Give it to Ralphie before you hurt yourself.
Thanks for the revolver. How much for the bourbon?

Chapter Sixteen: The Elsie Blues

If Annie could see me now.
Not the picture of her mother she'd expect.
Finally I might impress her.
Who'm I kidding?
She's never been able to stand me. Nothing I do will ever be of interest to Annie.
Sam's little girl all the way.
How stupid of me.
I thought going to work for Neil would impress her. Sam's best friend and a private detective.
Who better to find out what really happened to Sam- and who killed him.
More stupidity! If Neil's not drunk, he's on his way to getting drunk. Half his clients have left him.
And he blames Sam's death on Sam himself!
And he makes passes at his best friend's wife.
And even more humiliating, he doesn't remember making them.
And here I am bringing him a bottle of bourbon that nearly cost me my life at the hands of three goons sky-high on hop-
that I bought from a communist who screamed "Provocateur!" at me when I left his shop.
Sam, not even a dead husband should let that happen to the wife he loves.
I'll make a deal with you, Sam.
If I make it through this night alive, tell your daughter she has to respect me.

Chapter Seventeen: Car Chase

Neil!
Y'get the booze?
Y'took yer sweet time about it. They coulda skipped to Anaheim by now.
Elsie!
What's yer problem?
That ain't the way to behave!
Ha Ha Ha Ha Ha Ha Ha
Elsie! Come back!
VRROOOM

You comin'?
I don't have all day!
Neil! Look out!
They're headed back to Bay City!
You with me, or you gonna play games all day?
Useless! You know what you are? Useless!
You're swerving all over the place! Either drive or drink your bourbon, but you can't do both.
Save it f'church.
Neil, you're driving with your eyes closed! Are you all right?
Neil?
Diversionary tactic. They won' know I'm on their tail. Can't see too good inna a snow storm. Which car are we following?

Neil, you've got to get ahold of yourself!
There washa lil girl- hadda lil curl-
right inna mil of her forehead- An' when she wash good-
Neil! The light's changing!
You made me f'get! Washa lil girl- hadda lil curl-
In the mil of her forehead- primeval. An' when she was good- No, I dropped a line. Drop me a line shometime. Come up and shee me shometime.
Shtay in touch. An' when she wash good- she wash- What? What wash she? You never, never help! Yer ushelesh!

Lishen t'me.
I have a n'exshellin idea.

You drive.

Neil! Wake up! I don't know how to drive!
'seashy. Thish isha clutsh... thish isha ashelerata...
Thish isha lil girl- who hadda lil curl- right in the mil- the mil- mil- Down by the ol' mill stream-
Wake up!

TAXI!
Where you firsht met me- An my eyesh were blue- right inna mi'l of my forehead.

Four cars up!
That limo!
Follow it!

Follow that limo? I thought I heard 'em all, but on my mother's grave-

Now, follow that blonde- that one I got last month, right here on Main Street-

But it was Carole Lombard. You couldn't mistake her! Carole Lombard in Bay City! Window shopping! As if she needs to shop in Bay City.

"No!" I say t'myself, "It can't be her!" Small, tiny, but beautiful. Don't get me wrong, lady, you're nice looking too.

But Carole Lombard? I'm as close to her as I am to you. Except, I'm here in the front seat, and she's on Main, corner of Peach-tree.

Stop it! Stop it! Stop it!

Don't you recognize me, you stupid fool? I'm Jean Harlow!

Now, shut up and follow that limo!
No one's gonna believe me.

First, Carole Lombard and then Jean Harlow, what are the odds? Although in person, you don't look that much like her, but neither did Carole Lombard.

They stopped.
Someone's getting out.
Miss Harlow...
I don't need no trouble. OK, Miss Harlow?
Get out.
I have to go home to my daughter.
Get lost!
She's all I have in the world.
Where's your boyfriend?
Who hired him to tail us?
She needs me.
I know I'm gonna hate myself in the morning.
But I'll get over it.

Chapter Eighteen: 7 AM

Annie!
Annie!
Hello!
Are you up!
Here's breakfast!
Hello?
Annie!
What are you doing up here?
Explain yourself.

Chapter Nineteen: Casting Call

Next!
Thank you-
Next.
Next.
Thank you, very much.
Next!

M-may I-
have your name?
Neil!
I found her!
You jerk, I found her!
Cut it out! Can't you see I'm thinking!
The woman you want is in my office. Now you can go pass out again or pretend you're a detective.

Chapter Twenty: The Interview

About how tall are you?
Five-ten.
You look taller.
Men aren't comfortable with girls over six feet. I'm five-ten.
You look right to me, but I don't make the decisions. I'll need your name and address.
I'm across the street at the Hotel Flora, just passing through Bay City. I saw this line up of tall girls, and got curious.
Yeah? I may have something better for you. Can you type?
No.
You can learn. I'm looking for a kind of assistant.
What about my audition for the movie?
We'll work it out. But this is more steady. More permanent.
What sort of work?
I'll fill you in over drinks. I know a nice place we can have dinner. Where you staying?
The Hotel Flora.
Across the street?

I'm not free.
Change your plans.
This could be a real opportunity.
The audition?
What audition? What I have in mind...
Isn't this an acting job?
Lemme put this together. You got a nice deep voice. Low. Good on the telephone.
Mr.? What are you talking about?
Your future! Sky's the limit!
I'm leaving.
Big mistake. Meet me in an hour at the Hotel Flora bar. That where you're staying? I'm Neil Hammond. I'm a producer!
Directory
Hammond... Hammond... Here we go... Neil Hammond. Not a producer! A private detective!
Mae. Oh, Mae, oh, Mae!
Dumb little sister.
Better that you don't find me. For both our sakes.

Chapter Twenty-One: There Was a Little Girl

Something was goin'on between
us. I felt it. On the surface, you
could miss it . . . that she sees I'm
not like the others. I'm different.
Dangerous.
She makes fools of the other.
But not me.
She's big. But I'm plenty enough
man for her.
Looking down on me. Who does
she think she is? Where does she
get the nerve?
I come up with a decent offer,
cards on the table. And what's the
first thing she says?
"I can't type."
Who can't type these days? Every
broad, she wants a job, types.
Trust me, she types.
Mocking me that way.
She was mocking me. When I'm trying to
give her a break.
I start her out typing- The time come, I
promote her- To my assistant. After that,
what's to stop her?
Nothing!
We get married!
A kid or two. My mother had five
us. What's the matter with five?
Five kids, that should cut her do
to size. Looking down her nose
me that way.
She thinks she can play me? N
broad plays me!
Here's how it goes down. OK?
don't show up for that drink at
Flora.
That'll put a crimp in her style
Who'm I kidding?
She won't show either.
She won't show.
She was never gonna show.
Whore!

Chapter Twenty-Two: Right in the Middle Of Her Forehead

You found her.
That I did.
Have a drink.
What Now?
I have $2,500 in my purse-
that I will turn over to you.
$2,500?
And another 2,500 waiting for you after you complete the job.
The job?
What job?
Holy crap!
Ha Ha Ha Ha Ha Ha!
This is a gag, right?
We'll make it $3,000 as a down payment.
Lady, I don't even know your name, and you're asking me to perform last rites? Not that I have any moral objection-
But I'm a P.I. I never pulled a finale before.
Huh! But wouldn't that get her attention!
She thought she had me all figured out.
I'll come back later for your decision.
Wait! Pay me off completely now!
Tomorrow the bitch is dead.

Chapter Twenty-Three: A Night at the Flora

OTEL
FLORA
BAR
Tom Collins.
We don't get many unescorted single gals.
A few years ago I wouldn't be serving a single gal unescorted, but now- since they up and gave you gals the vote, anything goes.
You're so big, maybe they gave you two, three votes. No stoppin' you gals these days, am I right?
Another?

My panties?
You came here to kill me . . . but first you try on my panties?

Chapter Twenty-Four: Right in the Middle of His Forehead

Stupid of me.
To think I could be in the movies.
I'd be easy to find.
Even you could have found me.
Eventually, you'd sober up.
She'd make you try again.
Mansh gotta job t'do.
Down by the ol' mill shtream... Gotta job t'do.

Mansh gotta do his job.
Shweedheart, did you find my gun?

Yes.
I found it.
BLAM

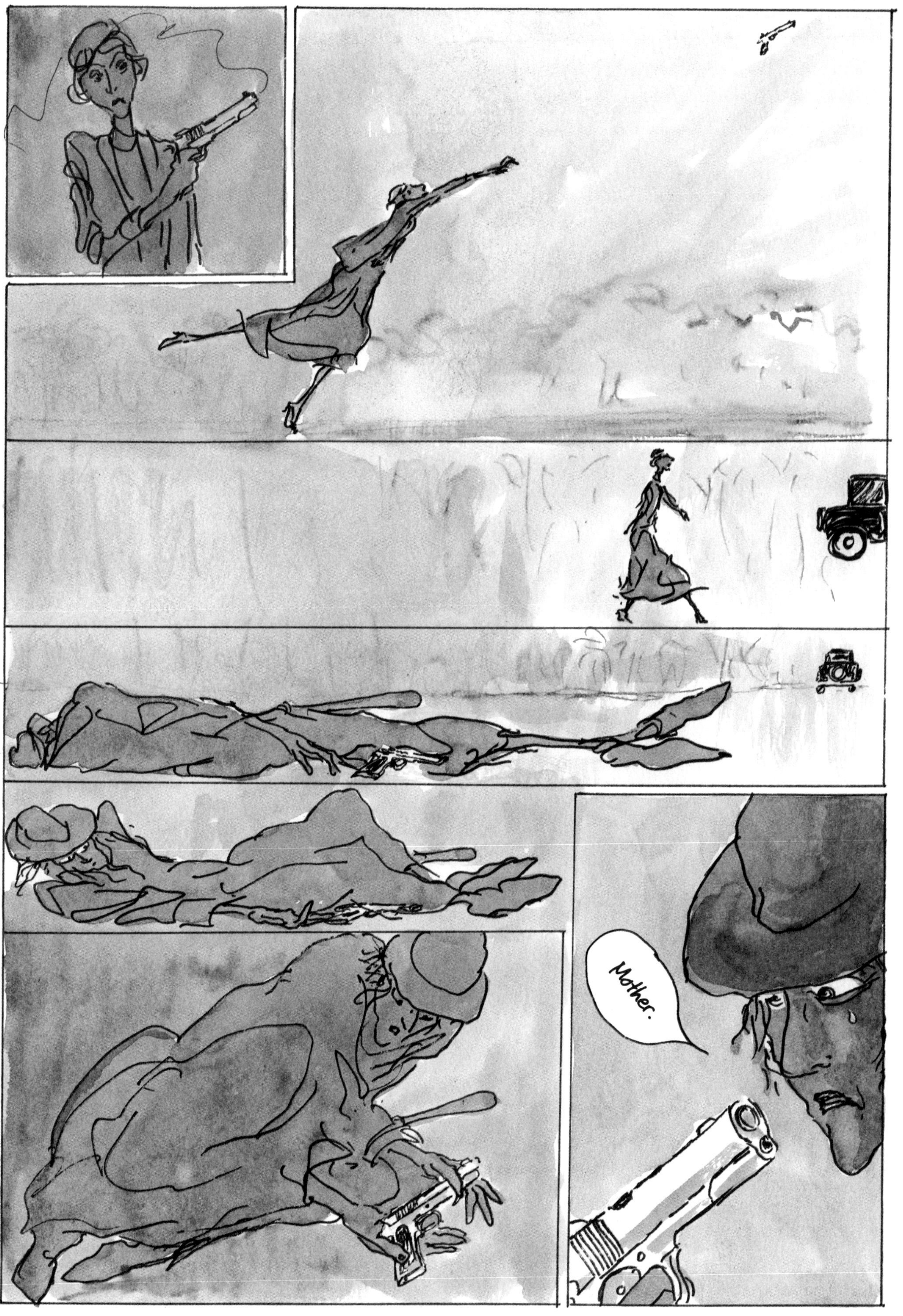
Mother.

She killed my mother.
Shut up.
It didn't happen.
I refuse to remember.
They can't make me tell them if I don't remember.
I was always the responsible one in the family.
Can't make them trick me,
make me talk.
Somebody you love
shoots someone else you love.
Every word I speak causes damage.
Can't be tricked if I never say another word.
If I never speak again, I can't tell them anything.
Never speak.
Silence!
But I can sing.
Singing is my life.
What harm if I sing?
BAY CITY BLUES..

Think you're gonna win-
You're bound to lose.
scared to face the news-
So I drink to confuse.
Got them on-again, off-again
Bay City Blues!
Happiness is a trick, it's a ruse-
'cuz comin' right atcha is them-
Bay City Blues!
Them awful, god-awful-
curl yer toes in yer shoes-
Make you pay, pay, pay so much more than yer dues, comin' to gitcha- is them Bay City Blues!

Part Two:

Hooray for Hollywood 1943

Chapter One: "Shut Up, Artie!"

The following broadcast was electrically transcribed as a special presentation of the Armed Forces Radio Network.
From Hollywood, California, we bring you the new comedy sensation from writer-producer Ann Hannigan, the show that has all America shouting:
"Shut Up, Artie!" CLAP CLAP CLAP CLAP CLAP CLAP
"Artie, Artie! Is that you up on the roof of our house?"
"No, Mom, it's not me. It's a bird, it's a plane, it's super-Artie!"
Ha Ha Ha Ha Ha Ha Ha Ha
"Artie, you come down this minute. You know you're afraid of heights."
"Mom, I know I'm afraid of heights, you know I'm afraid of heights, but Homer, my parakeet doesn't know I'm afraid of heights."
Ha Ha Ha Ha Ha Ha

"And Homer got out of his cage, Mom — and flew up here on the roof — and I crawled up here to get him down — but Mom, Mom! Who's gonna get **me** down?"

Ha Ha Ha Ha Ha Ha Ha

I wanna come down! I'm scared t'come down! Wanna, scared t' — wanna, scared t' — " HA HA HA HA

"Oh, shut up, Artie!" HA HA HA HA HA HA

HA HA HA HA HA HA HA HA HA HA HA

BLAM! BLAM! BLAM!

They can't resist the radio.
Fall for it all the time.
It's the laughter that gets 'em.
In the jungle . . . the sound of a radio audeience laughing . . .
I feel it too. You gotta go see what it is. Right, Captain?
Artie, Artie! Y'hear it, Captain? The kid in the show has the same name as you?
Don't forget to retrieve the radio, Corporal.
How much more do you expect me to take, Annie?
You're my real enemy. If I had you in my sights –
—I wonder what I'd do.

Chapter Two: Little Sammy Hannigan

I hate you!
I hate you!
Now, now, Sammy. Maria is here, Maria is here.
No! I don't want you! Go 'way! Go 'way!
There, there, Sammy, you be a good boy, and Maria will call Mommy as soon as she gets to Reno.
I don't want her! I hate her! I want my Granny! Granny! Granny!
Pinnacle Studios
Department of Image Security and Maintenence
Elsie Hannigan
Executive Vice President
Yes, Maria. What is it this time?
Reno? What in the world is Annie doing in Reno?
Never mind. Tell Sammy that Grandma is on her way.

Chapter Three: Lady Veil

And now, what you've been waiting for: the mysterious lady who's been causing so much talk in this, her premiere engagement. Let me introduce the Shadowy Songstress, the Divine Diva of Melodious Magic . . . Put your hands together for Her Royal Shyness –
ROOST
RENO ROOST
Lady Veil!
You told me you were leaving, Why are you still here? Isn't that you down the street? I see you everywhere. In our favorite bistro, I hear your conversation, Should I approach to say "hello"? I can't . . . the hesitation. I cross the room, But it's not you, You're not the one who's there,
She is fantastic!
Shut up, Ricky!

Five tables down I hear your voice,
I hurry over, what's my choice?
But it's not you, I find that queer,
Especially since I Know you're here.
Gin in my room, feelin' blue,
Trying to make one minus one make two,
You never told me what went wrong,
We never parted, not one "so long,"
How could you vanish without a trace,
Leaving an emptiness I can't face,
Out of my life, you're everywhere,
I can't take it, disappear!
No, I don't mean it,
stay, my dear.
Annie – Annie! What the hell's going on with you, Annie?
Who does she remind me of? I've got to meet her!
... Something tells me that I have met her.

Where did she disappear to?
Ricky, I tell you, I know her!
But how can it be?
How can she sing?
She couldn't talk, not a word!
Am I crazy?
But who else looks like that? so tall?
If it wasn't for that damned veil!
We've got to come back!
Nuts! Why do I let you do this to me? You're nuts, Annie!

Chapter Four: Little Orphan Sammy

NO! NO! NO! NO! NO! NO!
Maria, how long has he been going on like this?
Long time.
There, there, Sammy. Granny's here.
Granny! Granny!
Have you been able to reach Annie?
Granny! Granny!
Still he cry. "You're not my momma, you're not my momma," he say.
Does that ever sound familiar.
Sammy, Granny has to go back to business, but I'm coming back, and I'll be with you tonight, and tomorrow, and until Mommy comes home.
All right, my little munchkin?
His daddy? Maybe you call his daddy?
Granny!
WHAT?
Stupid Maria!
Da-da?

Chapter Five: Eddie Longo, Take 1

LONGO
Dancing Corporal
Action
Baby, hold my hand, Daddy's doin' the two-step –
Marchin' off to war, A red, white, an' blue s step –
Our last dance, A sweet me and you step, While I'm gone, Not one misstep, Take no false step, stay true blue –
To our tried and true step–
Keep the beat, need I repeat? We'll win the war, And dance lots more –
Doin' the American Boy and Girl, Give it a final twirl two-step!

Cut it! Print it! That's for Keeps!
Mae...
Well, if it isn't my little friend, the cleaning lady.
Did you find out who was writing those letters to Eddie, cleaning lady?
All taken care of, Mae. No more letters, no more blackmail threats.
Details?
No details. For five years I've been cleaning up the messes your husband and other bad boys and girls under contract to Pinnacle Pictures get themselves into —
The day I quit my job as the head of Image Maintenance is the day you and Eddie lose your free pass to Easy Street —
Because the day after that, I start looking into a ten-year-old murder back in Bay City, and investigate what connection you have —
— to the bully-boy bodyguard, Gaffney, and my boss, Neil Hammond, whose body was found in Deidrickson Park in women's panties and a bullet in his head.
You are delusional — but irritating. Don't irritate me, little girl. It will lead to consequences.

Chapter Six: Eddie Longo, Take 2

Eddie?
Are you home?
You ran off so fast, I didn't have a chance to tell you how incredible your number was, sweetheart.

Oh, Eddie, no!
Not again!
You should have believed in me more, Mae. I could have been a major star. Not just a B-star of low-budget musicals.
All I ever wanted was for you to believe in me.
Eddie, I do! I do!
I could've been welterweight champ!
You tried to talk me out of that fight!
Eddie, you nearly got yourself killed!
Because I was showing off for you! I wanted you to admire me! I had him beat, Mae! I never saw the punch coming!
Eddie, who picked you up and brought you out here to Hollywood? Who put out for a bunch of asshole producers so they'd give you a break?
Who pays off all your hookers, and not a single complaint?
B-hookers!
For a B-star of B-budget musicals, is that what you're asking me to settle for?
WHACK!

This? This is what I get? What more do you want, you ungrateful creep?
Real stardom!
That's what I want! A big-budget film! They're casting "Terminal Triumph," Mae. I read the book. The part of "Laughing Boy" is like written for me!
I'll be nominated! It will make me a major star! Not just a tap dancer, but a real actor!
Ha! Ha! Ha! Ha! Ha! Ha! Ha!
You sorry little asshole!
Wake up!
The studio is about to announce Hugh Patton for "Laughing Boy." He's big, he's sexy, his last picture grossed more than your last three combined!
What in God's name do you expect me to do? Shoot him in the head?
How about a coma? Would a coma satisfy you?
I don't say you have to go that far. Just find a way to . . . disable him. A bad fall? A broken back? A fractured skull?
Don't make fun of me, Mae. Call Gaffney. Get him down from Bay City. He's up to the job.
You put Hugh Patton into a coma, and I'll know you believe in me.

Chapter Seven: Hollywood Canteen

Hollywood Canteen

Barbara Stanwyck just walked in!

Am I crazy or was that Betty Hutton?

I saw Hugh Patton go in.

Did you see him in "Whispering Nights"?

He's gorgeous!

Relax, Miss Hannigan. I'm not as bad as the stories you've heard.

I'm hired to kill those stories, Mr. Patton. And the funny thing I found in checking them out, is that not only were they false, but most of them came from **YOU**.

I could get you fired for that lie, even if it **is** true.

My job is to protect you, not expose you. What I don't understand is why you go to all that trouble? You make me work very hard to hide facts that don't exist.

Isn't that Hollywood for you? Come have a drink with me afterwards, and I'll confess everything.

More lies?

Of course.

Will I be fired if I say no?

I can tell you're having too much fun with me to say "no."

I'm speechless.

Then you can't say "no."

Chapter Eight: "Shut Up, Artie!" 2

Don't touch that dial, America!
KDKY
From Hollywood, it's time for the show with those three special words you've been waiting all week to hear!
In trouble, Artie? Again? Goodness me, what happened this time?
Honest to galoshes, I didn't do anything this time, Sally. Last time, maybe, but not this time.
HA HA HA HA HA HA HA HA
I didn't do anything! Anything at all!
It's "SHUT UP, ARTIE!" The show that asks the question, "Will Artie ever shut up?"
Oh, shut up, Artie!
Yes! For all you folks at home, and our brave fighting men overseas—
NOOOOOOOOOOO

Annie—
The sponsor wants to see you right after the broadcast.
Did you hear that audience applause?!
Last week Crossley rated us just three points behind "Burns and Allen"!
Sit down, Annie, we may have a problem.
Problem? C'mon! A year ago no one ever heard of us!
Annie . . . do you know, or have you ever been associated with a Captain Arthur Folsom, U.S. Marine Corps?
Artie? You're kidding! He actually made captain? How could we possibly be winning the war?
Love your wit, Annie.
But this time, it's misplaced.
Captain Folsom is in combat on a South Pacific atoll, in the midst of heavy fighting, where pockets of resistance remain a threat.
Impossible!
Wait till I get my hands on that little twerp!
He's right in the middle of it.
Attorneys for Captain Folsom have filed a lawsuit against Touchstone Tobacco for libel, slander, and defamation of character.
Your little twerp is a twice-decorated war hero, Annie.

Annie—Unless this situation is resolved—
And soon!
We're going to have to take "Shut Up, Artie" off the air.
What are you saying?
You can't!
It's not possible!
I've been waiting for this all my life!
I've created a hit show!
I get 500 letters a week!
It's what I've always known; you work hard to get what you want.
And they work just as hard to take it away!
Artie! Artie! It's you, Artie!
SLAM
You'll be a dead war hero once I get my hands around your throat.
Ricky, pick me up in an hour, OK? OK?
As soon as I make some arrangements for the Kid, you're taking me to Reno.

Chapter Nine: Elsie's Drunk Scene

You're trying to get me drunk.
That's it, isn't it?
I'm right, aren't I right? Isn't that what you're trying to do?
Oops!
My glass is—
Empty. We can't have that.
No, we can't.
We can't and we shan't!
I drink—obviously!—I'm drinking now, but I wouldn't call myself a drinker. This is my first time in a month. I drink, but I drink sparingly. Do you know what I mean by sparingly? I don't drink to excess.
I had a boss who drank to excess. And he was murdered.
An unsolved crime. He was a private investigator.
It would be stupid for me to say that drinking to excess was the cause of his death. No. Not at all. It was a bullet to the head.
Did I tell you my husband was murdered too?
I think I know who did it.
Not my husband's murder, my boss. This blonde, her husband's right here. In the movies.
Do you think drinking makes me morbid?
I don't want you to think I'm morbid. I want you to like me.
That's why I took this job. To keep my eye on the blonde. And dig up evidence. Nothing, absolutely nothing so far. Don't you find that sad?
I don't want you to feel sorry for me.
Men don't like women they pity. I can't believe how relaxed I feel. Did you get me drunk at midnight by the swimming pool at your beautiful movie-star house, so I'd talk crazy this way? Tell me the truth.
But you're a movie star. You never tell the truth.

I thought I was immune to movie stars, you know, I'm around so many, and they're not as nice as you, or nice at all. Or even, if they act nice—it's their job to act as nice as they have to, to get what they want.
And my job is to pretend I believe them. I-I-I can't tell you how amazingly at ease I feel with you. Amazing! Absolutely amazing! I wish—you know what I wish? I wish **YOU** could be as much at ease.
But you're never at ease. Are you? At least that's my impression. First impressions tell you a lot. Do you want to know what's my first impression of you?
Tell me.
My first impression of you is, what does it mean that I'm the only one out here naked?

Chapter Ten: Veil Unveiled

Don't ask me if it's him,
I'll cry if you ask me,
Don't remember if it's him,
could've been.
Too much gin, don't ask me.
I Knew it!
I Knew it!
It's her! It has to be!
Baby-
I Know it's her, Ricky!
Don't ask me if we're through,
I don't ask you what you do,
Now I've done what you have done,
And I've lost, but have you won?
She's spotted me!
She's looking right at me!
I've tried your kind of fun,
Lost the stars, will I lose the sun?
Don't tell me.
I won't let her get away, again!
Sit down, Annie! Can I pick 'em or what?

Let me in! It's me, Annie! You saved my life!
You're not allowed back here, mister—lady—
Annie, this is nuts!
I've looked high and low for years! I hired private detectives!
I can't lose you again!
I'm gonna have to call the cops.
Let me help change your mind, friend.
I'm begging you—
CLICK
SLAM

Chapter Eleven: Anything You Want

You don't have to talk, just listen to my offer.
I live in a seven-room house in Santa Monica. With a pool. A mile from the pier. The beach. The ocean.
Your room will look out on the pool. We can go shopping. Anything you want.
I have a five-year-old son, Sammy. You'll like him. He's adorable, I know you two will be pals.
I can't lose you again! What do you care, Reno or L.A.? Plenty of clubs in L.A. that will book you. Ricky has connections. Right, Ricky?
Annie, what the hell are you doing?
Ricky can get you a job in any club you like. Movie stars will come: Van Johnson, Lana Turner, John Garfield. Anything you want!
Tell her, Ricky!
Annie, this is getting creepy.
Shut up, Ricky!

Chapter Twelve: Tiny Tim

Ten years, Gaffney. Keeping yourself busy?
Not so busy I didn't stay up nights, waitin' for your call.

Long hot drive from Bay City. Mind if I go in for a swim?
Suit yourself
Gaffney! What the hell are you doing?
Not a word from you and Eddie all these years. Dropped me cold. Never invitin' me down for the high life.
And me havin' to nickel-and-dime it all these years you forgot me.
It made me feel bad. Then out of the blue, you get in touch.
"What's goin' on?" I have t'ask myself, Mae and Eddie seen the error o' their ways? Or do they need a special job they can't trust to nobody but their old pal, Gaffney?

First off, you an' me go shopping for new duds at maybe some fancy Beverly Hills store that Tiny Tim can't even get in the front door—
Without Mae sashaying me in with her pocket book.
And After that, you fill me in on this job that's gonna make me rich, and forgive and forget. And you and me and Eddie will be best friends again.

Chapter Thirteen: The Kiss-Off

You're gonna love it here!
Hey! Remember me?
What are you doing in the car, Ricky? Come on in!
You come to Ricky for a change, Annie.
Ricky, this is no time to be difficult.
Ricky, I don't have time for your acting up, I have a house guest!
I try to go along, but you keep raising the ante!
Annie, I signed on as your boyfriend, not as a member of your staff!
You don't even know what I do for a living, do you?
Why is that so important right now?
Come into the house, and later, if you want me to play guessing games, I'll be happy to do it!
Screw you! I'm an agent!
What a disappointment. All this time, I thought he was a gangster.

Chapter Fourteen: Dressed to Kill

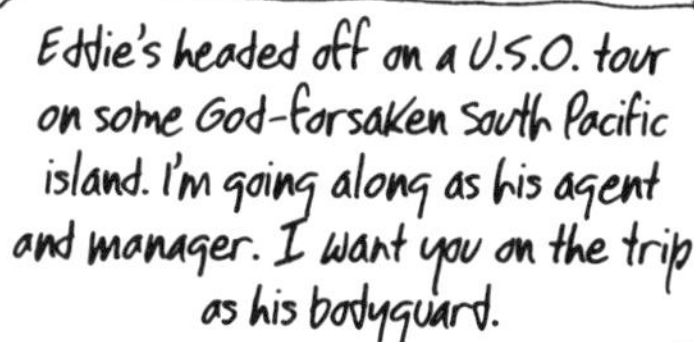
Eddie's headed off on a U.S.O. tour on some God-forsaken South Pacific island. I'm going along as his agent and manager. I want you on the trip as his bodyguard.

Whadaya think?
Another star on the trip is Hugh Patton. He's hot right now. He's up for the lead in a film Eddie wants real bad. You've seen him?
I don't go to pictures.

My Eddie and Hugh Patton hit this town the same time. You know Eddie, he's a party boy, an open book. But Hugh Patton he doesn't socialize. Doesn't go to parties. I've never met him. He's a mystery man. The rumor is he's a pansy.
In three weeks, we go off on the tour. Before then, let's see what you come up with. Photos, affidavits, stuff we can take to the newspapers. So before Elsie Hannigan gets a chance to kill the story, it's bye-bye Hugh Patton. And Eddie gets the part.
What if he's not queer? Or I can't prove it?

Then off we go to entertain the boys. Into a war zone. Where accidents happen. Hugh Patton's a big, big guy. An easy target for some sniper in the jungle. Not a fatal wound. Just bad enough to keep him out of action six months, a year.

Almost tragic, when you think about it. But it's all for Eddie, Eddie gets what he wants.
And I get...?

15,000 down front, another 35,000 when the job is done.
Makes me feel good that we're friends again, Mae.

Chapter Fifteen: A Song for Sammy

This is it, don't you love it? Not too big, but wait till you see the pool.
SAMMY! MOMMY'S HOME!
Go way! Go way! Go way! Go way! I want my Grammy!
Sorry, he can be a little high strung. Maybe he's reacting to your height.
Sammy, precious!
Sammy, I'd like you to meet— Goodness, we can't go around calling you Lady Veil, but I don't know your real—
A house in the woods, A house in the woods—
AIRPLANE!
A little boy lived In a house in the woods—

"Where is my mommy, Where is my daddy?"
The little boy asked in the house in the woods.
"Come find your mommy, Come find your daddy!" The little boy heard voices outside the house in the woods.
"Where are you, Mommy, Where are you, Daddy?"
Sang out the little boy in the house in the woods.
"Waiting, we're waiting, outside the door in the house in the woods."
"I'm afraid, I'm afraid to go outside of the house in the woods."
"Don't be, don't be afraid, Mommy and Daddy are waiting—
outside of the house in the woods."
She— she's just making it up— on the spot! And I can't believe how beautiful! A half hour! Saturday morning! A Radio show for kids!

Chapter Sixteen: Something for the Boys

Before I start shooting "Terminal Triumph" the studio booked me on a U.S.O. tour in the South Pacific.
So I've heard.
Eddie Longo's going, but he sings and dances. What the hell can I do?
Just be yourself.
You have no idea of how funny that is.
There are all sorts of rumors out there about why a big, strapping galoot like you isn't in the service. A U.S.O. tour will shut up the loud mouths.
Hey, what if I came along?
Too dangerous. The island's not completely secured.
C'mon! This town is every bit as dangerous, and talk about sneak attacks!
Pat, listen to me: it's been fifteen years since I've felt . . . anything for a man. Let me go with you.
Pat?
The hell with it!
The important thing—
is we be together.

Chapter Seventeen: The Ride to the Airport

The main thing, Annie, is you get Captain Folsom to drop all charges against the network.
And it's essential you get him to sign the release.
You don't understand! This is not the real Artie. He wouldn't do this to me!
Hugh, you look like you want to open the door, and jump out. Please, please, talk to me about this!
About what, Elsie? About what an absolute phony I am? Flying overseas to meet these legitimate heroes who risk their lives, **lose** their lives, get shot up—and I'm the one getting the red carpet treatment?
You see the size of that limo? Lookit, Mae! It's the god damned Twentieth Century Ltd! That's what Hugh Patton rates! For just two people! And you, me, and Gaffney, what do they assign me? A half-pint lime for their half-pint star!
That's over, Eddie! That's all going to change. I swear it!

Annie, this U.S.O. tour is mostly for the boys, our fight-ing men. That's why we're sending you!
But if your long friendship with Captain Folsom leads to talk of a settlement.
And he's willing to reason, we are autho-rizing you to make an offer.
This reputation I have as a loner . . . I like it! I like being a loner. Because when I'm not—that's when I'm in danger. Real life . . . contact with the real world . . . Kids who fight and die—if they knew the truth about this movie star—it's crazy! Insane! They'd run for the hills! You'd be leading the pack!
Shut up, shut up, Hugh! I can't stand you talking this garbage! You're the first good thing to come into my life in ten years! Why are you doing this?
I could name a dozen, a half dozen, half-pints in movies, bigger stars than Hugh Patton . . . Cagney's my size, almost exactly—Alan Ladd's almost a midget—Eddie Robinson—Astaire's a half-pint, would they stick him in a limo this size? Bullshit!
They didn't ask Astaire to go on this tour, Eddie, they asked YOU! And what you're going to show 'em, trust me, Ed-die, Astaire won't be able to carry your tap shoes.
I seen him in a picture once. He looked queer. One thing about you tap dancing, Eddie: you don't look queer.

Feel him out. An opening offer of $15,000. Probably more money than your Artie has seen in his lifetime.
I know he'll want to be reasonable. Look at what we're offering. We can pull a few strings, get him back home on leave . . . publicity! His picture on the papers . . .
If you have to, go up to $25,000. Not a penny more. Are you listening, Annie?
You think I'm going to negotiate with that little twerp? I'm gonna make him beg! I'm gonna make him apologize! Then I'll shoot him dead!
Lookit, they pulled in right behind us. I'm gonna wait him out, Mae. Let Hugh Patton get out of his limo first, and come over here and say hello.
If he thinks I'm going over to his limo, and I'm the first to say hello, he's got another think coming.
If I have to wait him out this whole trip, Mae, I'm not gonna be the one who says hello first. You watch, I won't do it!
I can't listen to this! I'll quit my job! I'll leave town! Pat, I can't do this!
Elsie, Elsie, what have I done? I'm a coward and a jerk and I'm going to get past this—this idiocy. Because of you! Because of **YOU**! I have to; the best thing that's ever happened to me, and what do I do? Forgive me, Elsie, I should be shot! But not for 25 or 50 years—till I have a chance to make it up to you!

Chapter Eighteen: Artie's War

Men, you can see behind me this stage being constructed. It's for the U.S.O. performers who are flying out from Hollywood to entertain our troops here on Tarawa. These actors and singers and dancers don't know what might be facing them when they get here. If they did, they might cancel the trip.

Now Tarawa has been secured, but there are still pockets of resistance—diehards—hiding out in the jungle, and they have more places to hide than we know where to look for them. W can't let them get away with that, can we?

Noooooooooooo!

So that's where this plan of mine com in. I don't have official permission for us to act on it. You'll all have to volunte I can't order you to sit in the audience tomorrow night, enjoying the show like you don't have a worry in the world. Laughing, applauding—w the enemy out there—these diehards lurking in the jungle—**also** watchin the show—

Right, the show must go on. You men have fought hard and won hard, and now it's your right to get a look or two at some of these Hollywood stars—some of them of draft age who somehow—for some reason—were never called up to serve their country.

Boooooooooo!

Yeah, I bet they feel just awful about it. So I came up with a plan to—just maybe—give these boys a chance to experience—maybe, just maybe—what you leathernecks have been going through.

And if they're out there—and my guess is they won't be able to resist this U.S.O. per formance: a brightly lit stage, singers an dancers right there in the spotlight, and cheering, applauding audience of unprepa marines . . . what they'll see is sitting duc You will all be sitting ducks!

Noooooo!

Damn right, no! My bet is that the enemy is going to find you sitting ducks irresistible. And they will come out of hiding. They will attack. What they will not know is that, as you sit in the audience, hidden under the benches you sit on, secured in narrow trenches covered with dirt and brush, Is buried an arsenal of automatic weapons.
And hidden in the palm trees surrounding the stage, will be 25 snipers, waiting for these guerillas to be suckered in by the bright lights and music, and pretty girls dancing.
YAAAAAAAAAY
No question, my plan will involve some risk for the U.S.O. personnel onstage, but we are going to make it our business to see that this turns into nothing more than a good story they can tell the folks back home. And if they take a casualty or two, they will have done it, just like you, in the service of their country.
Men, if this plan works, all of us will share in the credit. And if it fails, some of you will testify as witnesses at my court-martial.

Chapter Nineteen: Plane Talk

Annie—
Talk to me.
Please.
Well, look who dropped in from star-class to the cheapo writers' seats. It's Sammy's grammy.
You've been mad at me your whole life, and I've never understood why.
I've come to accept the bad feeling between us, but what I can never accept—because it breaks my heart—is to see the same explosive anger repeating itself with you and Sammy.
No sale, Elsie. Your nicey-nice act has done wonders for you at Pinnacle Pictures, but you can drop it with me. You just make yourself look ridiculous, Elsie.

I hate it when you call me Elsie.
I am not your friend. And I refuse to be your enemy. I am your mother.
That's a laugh! You were never my mother. You were more of a mother to Artie than to me!
Because he let me.
Artie accepted and appreciated mothering. You scorned it. And let me remind you, since we're speaking of Artie, this is a U.S.O. tour we are on—
It's been six years since you've seen Artie. He's been out there fighting a war. When you see him, don't you start another one.
Still watching out for Artie. Well, he's gonna need it. How come you never watched out for me?
What?!
Do you know how many times I've wished you dead?
A hundred times a day? A thousand?
Do you have any idea how many fantasies I have had about killing you?
Pushing you in front of a bus—out a window—poisoning your coffee—smothering you in your sleep—sticking a knife in your back—
What's this, Elsie in tears?
Elsie and her famous feelings! For me? No, for herself! Elsie is too busy feeling her own pulse, so she has no time to feel for her daughter—her alleged daughter.
Enough of this crap. I have a comedy sketch to write for Artie and the boys, so please, weeping Elsie, get the hell out of my sight.

Pathetic.

Mrs. Longo—
This man asleep in front of you, I recognize as Gaffney, your bodyguard in Bay City ten years ago, who knocked me unconscious.

Marine Command in Tarawa will be curious to know why Eddie will need his own bodyguard in a base protected by the U.S. Marines.
Or have you assigned Gaffney **other** duties on this tour?

The protection Eddie is going to need will be back home, because I am through cleaning up the scrapes he gets into before the press finds out! You are on your own.

Wuz happening?
Nothing that concerns you. Go back to sleep.

Chapter Twenty: The Island

I want to welcome you to the newly liberated island of Tarawa. I am Captain Folsom.
Artie!
I'd never know you! You're twice the size I remember you!
I'd know you! Younger and prettier than ever! Am I old enough to call you by your first name?
Artie?! No! That can't be Artie! It's impossible!
Mae, do something! Look at the greeting Elsie Hannigan gets, and she's a nobody! And Hugh Patton is right down front by her side, and where am I? In the rear of the whole goddamn U.S.O. tour! Whose side are you on, Mae?
I'm sure you've all got questions, and I will try to answer them all when we get to the theater area!
If you pile into the transport, over there with your gear, we've got a nice, bumpy ten-minute ride to the outdoor stage, and then to your quarters nearby!
Isn't he going to say "hello"? Isn't he going to even look at me? Is it possible he's an imposter? It's some kind of trick, Artie didn't have any muscles! Do I hear laughing? Is somebody laughing at me?
Ha! Ha! Ha! Ha!
Ha! Ha! Ha!

Your performance is scheduled for tonight at 1900 hours. I can assure you that everything is being done to ensure your safety.
But pockets of enemy resistance, although they are small in number, are still active in this area.
Mae! What the hell have you got me into? This isn't what I signed up for!
Shhh, baby. Mae's gonna handle it.
A trapdoor has been built into the stage. At the first sign of a problem, any problem at all, it will spring open, and personnel onstage will evacuate through the trapdoor onto a thick bed of leaves that will cushion your fall.
Artie, I'm staring straight at you! Artie, why do you refuse to look at me?
Full evacuation will only take seconds, and our men will be on alert around the perimeter of the stage to cover your every move.
He acts so sure of himself! Artie, in real life, isn't that way at all!
Forgive the interruption, Captain Folsom, I am Hugh Patton.
I recognize you, sir.
I think I speak for everyone here when I tell you that we are not here to make problems, but to put on a show that will take your mind off your problems. Gratefully and humbly, we are here to serve you by entertaining you. And we consider that our duty and our privilege.
YAAAAAY!

I'm on the next goddamned plane out of here!
You little jerk!
Do you or don't you want that part that Hugh Patton is up for?
I could get shot at, Mae!
Only if you're lucky! You see that big lug? He's better looking and more manly than you are!
Because if they don't, who the hell is going to notice you?
Where did Artie go?
So you better hope and pray they start shooting at you doing your dancing act!
Elsie!
Have you seen Artie?
He was onstage a minute ago!
Don't pretend you don't hear me!
She was never any help to me before, why expect it now?
Artie! Are you hiding from me?
Stop behaving like a child! Come out of the jungle, Artie!

Chapter Twenty-One: The Audience

Artie, I'm expected onstage to make some opening remarks in a little while.

You know that!

So I can't go on playing this stupid game with you!

Ha Ha Ha Ha Ha

Who's laughing?

Artie, are you hiding out here with a bunch of marines, ordering them to laugh at me?

Ha Ha Ha Ha Ha Ha Ha Ha Ha

That's cruel, Artie! I won't stand for it!

It sounds like a studio audience at a radio broadcast . . .

Oh, shut up, Annie!

Ha Ha Ha Ha Ha

No! You've got that wrong! It's "Shut Up, Artie!" Not Annie! Artie! It's Artie!

BOOOOOOOO

Who are you to boo me? I came all this way to entertain you!
HAHAHAHAHAAHA
Oh, shut up, Annie!
You! You shut up! I am out of patience!
No more U.S.O. tours for me!
Oh, shut up, Annie!
Ha Ha Ha Ha Ha Ha
I have to get back to go onstage, but after I do my four minutes—
Oh, shut up, Annie!
Ha Ha Ha Ha Ha Ha
– And here she is, the creator and writer of that comedy sensation, "Shut Up, Artie!"
I'm coming back out here, and I'll "Shut up, Annie!" you! The whole rotten bunch of you!
Miss Ann Hannigan!
I'd rather entertain the Japanese!
BOOOOOOOO

Chapter Twenty-Two: The Jungle Follies

I-I can not tell you how thrilled I am to be here.
Down in the audience . . . there he is . . . it's Artie!
I am often asked, is "Shut Up, Artie!" based on true life? Is there a real Artie? OK, let me tell you a story.
No, it's not Artie—or is it? He's gotten so big, he looks like all the rest of them.
A few weeks ago, I was serving drinks at the Hollywood Canteen, and a sailor came over—and he grabbed me—and he kissed me! On the lips!
And this sailor said to me, "Five minutes ago, Bette Davis grabbed me, and kissed me on the lips. She said to pass it on."
Is it him? Or not?
Ten minutes later, the same sailor comes back—and he grabs me—and he sticks his tongue in my mouth.
Did you see that, Pat? Mae's hired goon, Gaffney, just slipped off into the trees.
What's he up to?
And he said, "Esther Williams just stuck her tongue in my mouth—and she said, 'Pass it on.'"
No good is what he's up to.
I'll take a look.
A half hour later, the same sailor shows up, and he's stark naked!
Careful, Pat—he's dangerous.
So am I.

"Esther Williams, again? She took off all your clothes?" "No," the sailor said, "this time, it was Lana Turner!" And she said, "Pass it on!"

Yeah . . . this should do it.

Clear view of the stage.

When Hugh Patton comes up to the mike . . .

And then and there, that sailor was about to rip off my clothes—

Pow!

But lucky for me, two MPs were right there, and they grabbed the sailor. And, as they dragged him off, I yelled at him, "Pass it on!" HA HA HA HA HA HA HA HA HA

Now, the story I just told you is my answer to the question: is "Shut Up, Artie!" true-to-life? I'll explain: I write a radio comedy show. **Nothing** I write is true-to-life. If it was, I wouldn't be working in Hollywood.

We, in Hollywood, have nothing to do with the real world. That's **your** job. **Our** job is to show our thanks and our gratitude by singing and dancing for you—

You OK?

And tell jokes, and give you boys a true-blue American old-fashioned good time!

Better get out of here. There'll be others.
Jeez! Hugh Patton!
What are you doing out here?
You're a movie star!
They're moving in.
And now, it's my pleasure to introduce—
Those two wacky, zany clowns—you loved 'em in "Two Freaks in a Foxhole," Harris and Hamberg!
You saved my life—this is nuts!
Harris?
Yeah, Hamberg.
I don't wanna be here, Harris!
You don't wanna entertain the troops?
The troops aint the problem. I don't want to entertain the mosquitoes.
Artie!
There you are! Don't run away!
Hamberg, I was all geared up for this trip, so I wanted to do some research, so I went to some war movies: John Wayne in the South Pacific, also Dana Andrews, also Van Johnson—
Artie, why are you hiding from me?

I'm a different person now, Artie. And you are, too. And the new person you are has no right to hold a grudge—
Movie stars in a South Pacific film, you know what they do, Hamberg?
I'll bite.
No, Hamberg, it's the mosquitoes that bite! And all you see is these movie stars go—
SLAP! SLAP! SLAP!
—Against the different person I've become.
Movie stars in the South Pacific kill more mosquitoes than they kill Japs.
Hold it!
This is as far as you go.
Bug bites make me sick, Hamberg. I'm allergic!
Sit down, relax. You got till after dark.
Bug bites make me swell up. I shouldn't be in the South Pacific!
When it gets dark, they'll attack, and with all that shooting going on—
I could get a serious infection!
SLAP! SLAP!
—who's gonna investigate the death of a movie star, caught at the wrong place at the wrong time?

Mae put you up to this?
Where'd ya learn t'use a knife like that? Inna movies?
I kiss girls in the movies. I'm a romantic lead. The part with the knife was pure ad-lib.
Izzat what acting teaches you? To make it look natural? I shoulda took lessons. You're gonna be my first. I never knocked off anybody before.
Don't get me wrong. I killed people. No sweat. Three or four suckers, but I was only hired to beat 'em up, and they weren't up to it. Beatin' up suckers comes easy, but—
Remember I saved your life.
Good point. On the other hand, a lug like me being saved by a pansy, it's humiliating. Makes me look bad.
And comin' at ya right now, it's the Cliff Sterrett Orchestra!
The band of swing and cling will play that home-front favorite—
You're on next, Eddie. Here's your skimmer.
I'm not going on! Have a heart, Mae!
—"Don't Sit Under the Apple Tree."
You're going on, if I have to drag you, kicking and screaming—
—And don't think I won't!

Thank you, Cliff. And now a special treat—you've seen him fight in the ring—
Mae, if this is your idea—
Of giving me the support I need—
You've seen him dance in the movies! Here he is: Eddie Longo!
You're on, Eddie!
Play it, boys!
Eddie!
Don't just stand there!
Dance, Eddie!
What do you think you're doing?
I'm hot.
I'm sweating.
No tricks.
I'm just taking off my shirt.
See?

Keep playing the intro!
Eddie! You can't not do this! You've got to dance!
Your whole life, Eddie—it's about screwing up your big moments! But not this time!
I beg you, don't do this to us! I love you, Eddie!
Ma'am, I have to remove you from the stage.
I need to borrow this!
Hey!
Keep playing Eddie's intro!
Hugh Patton.
A girl.
Dance, Eddie!
You make it look worse and worse for me.
I can't kill a girl.
Maybe someday down the line—my fifteenth, twentieth kill—
Maybe then a girl, but—

Knocking you off was gonna be a step up for me.
I mean, Tiny Tim Gaffney dices a movie star! When the word got out, it woulda been my graduation day! No more beatin' up deadbeats. And lookit how you ruin it: bad enough a pansy should save my life, but a bimbo with a mustache? You make me a laughing stock!
Dance, Eddie, damn it!
BLAM!
Dance, you son of a bitch!
I'm dancing!
Look, Mae!
BLAM!
Give me that gun! Are you nuts?
Yea, yeah, yeah! I'm a dancing fool, Dancing hot! Dancing cool—
BLAM!
BLAM!
Hear that?
The attack!
It's begun!

Cuz I'm dancing for the USA, can you see?
Give me that gun!
Yes, Eddie! That's it!
Dancing day into night,
BLAM
By the dawn's early light—
BLAM
BLAM
BLAM
Jeez!
BLAM
BLAM
Soft-shoe and tap—
What the hell have you started?
Practice that victory lap—
BLAM
BLAM
BLAM
BLAM
You're doing great, Eddie!
Spring the trap!
Dancing hard as can be, For the land of the free—
BLAM
BLAM
BLAM
BLAM
BLAM
BLAM

Glad you heard my story
caught my struttin' to Ol' Glory—
You dance on their graves, Eddie!
BLAM!
BLAM!
BLAM!
The trap! The trap! Spring the trap!
Give me my gun!
BLAM!
BLAM!
Artie!
I know that's you! Come down from there!
BLAM!
A dancing fool is what I am—
Artie!
I swear you have nothing to prove!
You're breaking my arm, you son of a bitch!
BLAM!
Get down, Annie! Those are real bullets!
BLAM!
Put me down, you'll hurt yourself!
You've gotten even loonier, how is that possible?
Proud to be your dancing man—

Annie! Artie!
Elsie! Stay down!
Artie!
BLAM!
BLAM!
You're hit!
I'm OK! The trap door! Spring the trap door!
BLAM!
Catch my speed, dig my smile,
Dancing with a lot of style—
Goddamn thing won't open!
It worked an hour ago!
BLAM!

Let's move! Take this, I carry extra.
BLAM!
And put your goddamn shirt on, I can't stomach the sight of you!
BLAM!
BLAM!
I've got to get you out of—
Screw you! You think I'm gonna let you save me twice in a row? Lee'me be!
BLAM!
Back off, I told you!
You humiliate me one more time—
BLAM!
I'll forget you're a broad, and blow your head off.
BLAM!

Dancing fast as I can—
BLAM!
Where's Gaffney? He should've been back by now.
Gaffney!
—Cus I'm your Dancing Man—
It's all right you're suing me, Artie. Making fun of you on the radio— I didn't even mean it to be you. I just liked writing something with you name on it.
BLAM!
You and me and Sammy and Dorothea—
When we go home, Artie—
BLAM!
An awful lot of blood—
Remember that tall, tall woman who saved us from the store-cop in Bay City? Her name is Dorothea. She's living with us.
Medic! We need a medic here!
Where the hell is that son-of-a-bitch Gaffney?
He's unconscious, Annie! We need help!
He's only resting. You don't understand. He's a war hero. He has a right to rest, if he wants to.
BLAM!
BLAM!
Annie, there's something wrong!
And here's a surprise you're gonna love, Artie. Sammy! He's your son! You didn't know, Artie! Yes! You're a daddy!
This has to be more than a shoulder wound . . .

BLAM!
Hugh Patton!
BLAM!
Elsie!
BLAM!
Thank God!
Hugh!
Please, Elsie, shhhh—
Artie's asleep.
BLAM!
I've never actually met Hugh Patton—
So why do I think I know him?
BLAM!
Elsie, Artie and I need to be alone. Would you and your friend go somewhere else?
I'm sorry, Annie—
He's gone.
BLAM!
See how you fooled everybody, Artie? What a cool trick. It's time to open your eyes now.
BLAM!

There he is.
Big as life.
Hugh Patton.
Artie, listen, I'm going to count to three.
OK?
The man who thinks he's stealing my Eddie's part.
Annie—
And when I finish counting you'll open your eyes.
One—
OK, Artie?
If you want something done right—

Two—
Three!
BLAM!
He's down!
ELSIE!
MOMMY!

I got him!
I got him!
P'CHING!
I almost forgot—
There's another war on!
Gaffney! Where are you?
Zat you, Mae? Everything's fuzzy . . .
I'm shot up for keeps . . . Come closer . . . can't see too good . . .
Eddie's a dancing hero, Hugh Patton has a bullet in him, and you stayed alive just long enough for me to finish a perfect day.
BLAM!

Point blank, and you still can't finish the job . . . you incompetent . . .
Just thinka the honor, Mae . . . You're my First Lady!
BLAM!
Hunnh— I'm up!
Eddie!
Time to look after me! Hunnh— uhhunnh—
EDDIE!
It's your turn!
Hunnh
Uhhunnh
Hunnh
Uhhunnh
Caught one in the thigh . . . hunnh . . . Gotta make it out of here. Hunnh— uhhunnh—
BLAM!
Yeah, dancing, High-stepping, American fool!
BLAM!
Swinging out hot!
Swinging out cool

She's not dead! Tell me she's not dead!
She's my mother! Do you know she's my mother?
Got to get her treated.
Mommy's going to get treated! Did you hear that, Artie? She's not dead, and neither are you!
It's a head wound... Not good...
hunnh—urihunnh—
Eddie?
hunnh—
please, Eddie.
I... need... help... Eddie...
BLAM!
Lemme outa here!

I coulda been Killed!
Hunnh—
unhunnh—
hunnh—
unhunnh—
I coulda been Killed!
I coulda been Killed!
Hunnh—
unhunnh—
Eddie—
Mae!
You're never there when I need you.
I coulda been Killed.

I coulda been killed.
Hunnh Unhunnh—
I coulda—
Who's there?
Don't come any closer!
Hunnh unhunnh hunnh unhunnh—
I warn you—
Hunnh unhunnh hunnh.
I'm armed!
Unnh hunnh

hunnngh...
BLAM!
BLAM!
Unnngh...
hunnngh...
You were great out there, Eddie...
I... think... you'll get... the part...

Chapter Twenty-Three: Visit

Pat?
I'm here, Elsie.
I can't see.
The wound is to your right temple, it was glancing, and messy, and you're wrapped up like a mummy, but you're going to be fine.
Are you sure? Or are you just trying to make me feel better?
Yes, I'm sure. And yes, I'm trying to make you feel better.
Elsie, I intend to make you feel better for a long time to come.
Hugh Patton, what are you saying?
Elsie, when you get better, there are things about me you're going to learn about.
That sounds ominous. What things?
They're flying us out of here in the morning. We'll have plenty of time to talk, after you get some rest.
No!
Pat!
I want to know now! What things?
Pat?

Chapter Twenty-Four: Revelation

Mae—
It's Patty.
Patty?
Patty who?
It's dark, I can't see.
Is it my sister, Patty?
Have you come to kill me?
Give me a gun so I can finally give you what you deserve!
You've had plenty of opportunity. I've been right under your nose for a long time.
Just wait till I'm back on my feet! I'll kill the two of you, you and Dorothea! Did you think I'd let you get away with it?
You killed my mother!
You killed Mother. I tried to stop you.
NO!
She was having one of her breakdowns. She was crazy. She was beating you with a baseball bat.
No!
You put her up to it!

Mae, we raised you, Dorothea and I. We adored you. We protected you. From Mother!
The lies you spread! The picture-perfect Hughes twins! See how they care for their shrimpy, pathetic sister . . .
It was Mother who called you "shrimpy."
NO! She loved me more than she loved you!
You're beautiful!
My god, Mae, you were five foot eight when you were nine! And look how you grew up—
Stop mocking me! I'm a midget and ugly compared to you two!
Mother understood me! Mother protected me!
By beating you? If I hadn't grabbed that baseball bat—
She wasn't hurting me—
It was a game we played—
I was bad!
And then you grabbed the bat out of my hands. You hit Mother—
Then you went for her gun—you shot her twice!
No! You killed her! I will avenge her!

It's over! This insanity must stop!
Look at me, Mae!
You look—you look like—Hugh Patton.
It's so dark, I can barely see—
I'm finished with this masquerade!
Off comes the mustache!
You're Hugh Patton!
Not another second of this crap! Hugh Patton is a fake! Hugh Patton is your sister!
I'll expose you, Patty! You're not going to get away with this!
I'm done, Mae! It's over! Let Eddie have my part in the picture!
I'll tell the whole world! It will be the end of your career!
And not a moment too soon. More power to you, Mae.
Patty, wait! Don't walk out on me! Why are you doing this?
Is it because of me?
Are you sacrificing yourself for me?
Patty!
Patty!
I won't tell!
I'm sorry I tried to kill you, Patty!
I loved you best!

Chapter Twenty-Five: Flash!

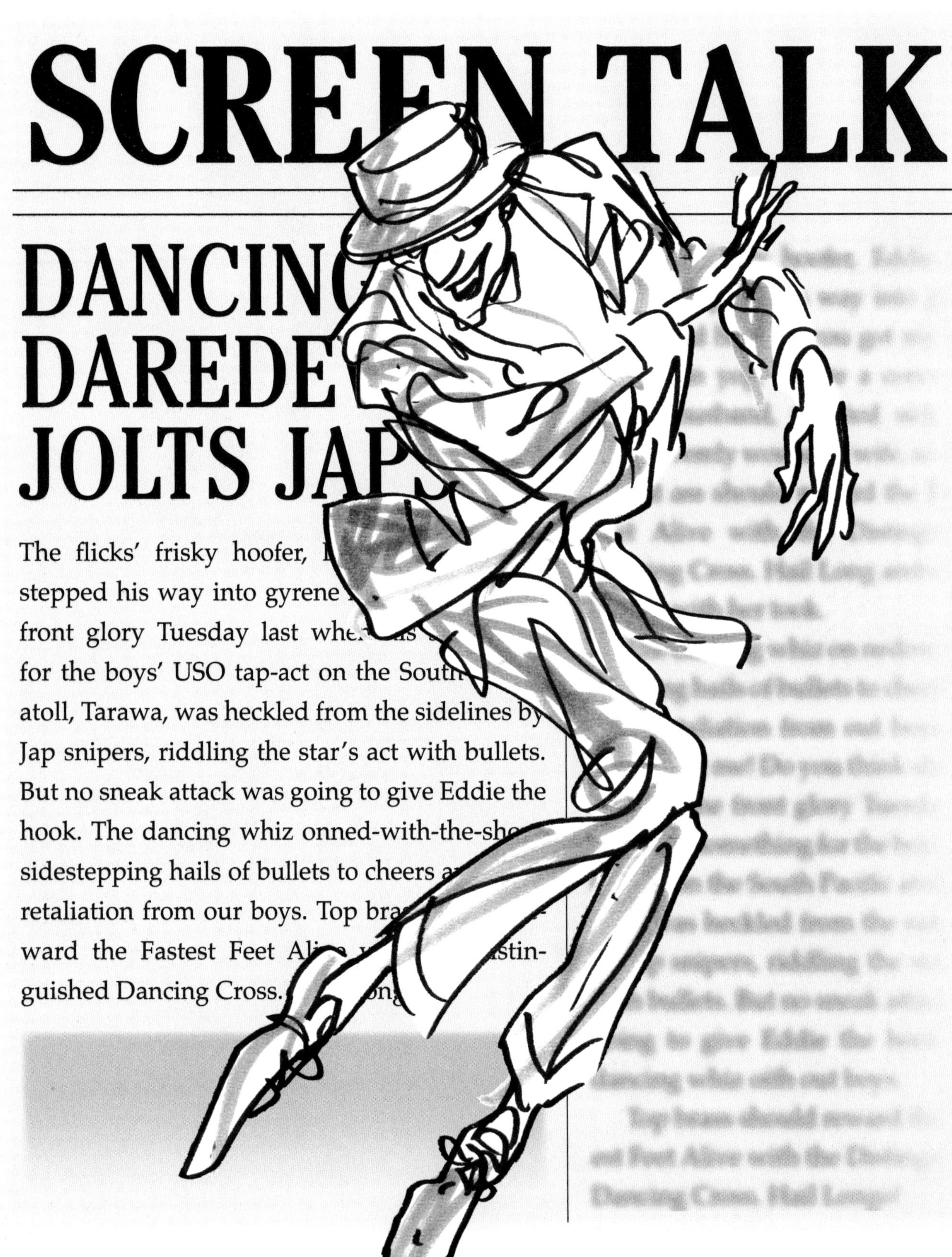

SCREEN TALK

DANCING DAREDE JOLTS JAP

The flicks' frisky hoofer, stepped his way into gyrene front glory Tuesday last whe for the boys' USO tap-act on the South atoll, Tarawa, was heckled from the sidelines by Jap snipers, riddling the star's act with bullets. But no sneak attack was going to give Eddie the hook. The dancing whiz onned-with-the-sh sidestepping hails of bullets to cheers a retaliation from our boys. Top bra ward the Fastest Feet Al stin- guished Dancing Cross.

Chapter Twenty-Six: Homecoming

We're home, Mother.
Over here, Eddie!
Eddie!
Eddie!
Eddie! Take off your hat and wave!
Eddie!
Eddie!
Eddie! It's me, Ricky Pastor!
I'm so glad you got my wire, Ricky, can you believe this turn-out?
I'm here for you, Eddie, but you gotta' cut the showboating!
You're a concerned, loving husband, worried sick over your severely wounded wife, so climb in that ambulance and go with her to the hospital!
But I'm a dancing war hero, Ricky!
Ricky is handling it, Eddie!
Trust me!
It's her eyes, Annie. Damage to the optic nerve. They don't know how serious—
Do you think she'll be all right?
I can take care of her.

No, I'm her daughter. She's going home with me! Dorothea and Maria and I will take good care of her.

Dorothea?

The girl who's come to live with me, who— it's funny, now that I look at you—

What happened to your mustache?

You look just like her.

Mr. Patton, are you all right?

I'll be back on my feet in no time, Eddie.

Mae, the word is out!

How I danced my way through an enemy attack. Did you see me? Everyone's looking at me different.

That termite, Ricky Pastor—

What was he doing at the airport, Eddie?

So much is happening, Mae. And with you laid up—

Till your back on your feet, Ricky's offered me a hand. I know this is hard for you—Ricky's getting me an audition for "Laughing Boy" in "Terminal Triumph."

That's my job, Eddie!

It's for the best, baby. You'll see. And you have my guarantee, I'm gonna see to it, Ricky works out a generous arrangement with you, you're gonna be thrilled.

You're shot up bad, Mae. I love you, but you said it a hundred times, I blow too many chances . . .

It's now or never, Mae. The big time.

Chapter Twenty-Seven: Kill My Mother

Mother, it's me, Annie! I know you can't see me.
I can hear you. Did you say, "Mother"?
We're home in L.A. You're safe, Mommy. The Medical Center. You're getting the best care available.
Nothing stays in my head. Did I hear you say, "Mommy"?
You could've been killed, Mommy. Artie is dead. Everything that happened is my fault!
Artie is dead? Oh, Annie— the poor boy!
I can't believe you're talking to me as if—as if you don't hate me.

It took a walk in the jungle, and you getting shot-
for me to figure this out . . .
I felt left out. And you and Pop were so close. I hated you.
And I hated you more after Pop got shot, and you went to work for that stupid private eye. I was sure you were sleeping with him. What I needed was a mother I didn't hate. Who would protect me. From you. So I invented one.
Tough, hard-boiled, mean enough to keep me from getting shot like Pop.
I called her Chelsea- the opposite of Elsie. Chelsea gave me a thumbs-up on everything rotten I wanted to do.
Lie, steal, manipulate, turn Artie into my slave-
Browbeat and humiliate you. Turn you into a full-time babysitter because I couldn't stand my baby. Because Artie was his father. Every dirty trick I pulled, Chelsea said "Atta girl!"
Then Artie got shot- and you got shot. And Chelsea whispered, "Better them than you." So I strangled her. Right there in the jungle where you were lying there bleeding.
I killed my fake mother to save my real mother. Only then did I learn how much I loved you-
Until you were shot, and could've been dying, I didn't know. And now- I don't understand how this works-
But I'll do anything I have to get you back.
Oh, Mommy, oh, Mommy, do I have a chance?
Don't ever stop calling me that.

Chapter Twenty-Eight: Hugh into Patty

Pat!
You're here!
Thank God!
I'm blind...
You are not blind.
You don't think I'm blind? What you think is so important to me.
I have something to tell you, Elsie.
You do think I'm blind! You don't want to see me anymore.
I don't blame you. That's all right. Don't feel bad. Annie and I—
Elsie, you have to let me talk. And after I finish, if you still want anything to do with me—
I do, I do want you! What are you saying?
What I'm saying is—
Elsie, I'm a woman.
...
...
...
Elsie?
Is this a joke?
I'm a woman, Elsie.
Don't be stupid!
Hugh Patton is an invention. I was on the run. Mae had been hiring people to kill me.
Who's Mae?
Mae Longo. She's my sister.
Mae Longo is **not** your sister!

Mae hired Neil Hammond to kill me.
MY Neil Hammond?
Before he could kill me—I killed him.
I'm delirious.
I was the one who killed your boss. But I knew Mae was not going to stop coming after me.
I had to go into hiding. I became a man.
I'm big. Bigger than most men. I can act. I can sound and move like a man.
Patty Hughes became Hugh Patton.
But you're a movie star!
An accident.
I auditioned for a small part—and somebody noticed me.
I'm Patty Hughes. Patricia Hughes. Patty!
No you're not! You're Pat! My Pat! You're Pat!
I'm sorry. I'll leave now.
What do you mean? How dare you bring my whole world crashing down on my head, and leave?
You will not leave!
Elsie, I am so sorry.
Sorry isn't the half of it! He's sorry!
She's sorry. Patty is sorry.
Are you still six foot two? Or is that also a lie?
I am still six foot two.
No mustache?
Nope.
I'll miss that mustache.

You have tits, I suppose.
Yes.
That's why you never undressed, or let me touch you intimately. I assumed it was some movie star I-don't-like-to-be-touched affectation, and it might take years for me to wear you down.
Big tits or little tits?
In-between.
Oh, dear!
What?
I like small tits.
Elsie...
We'll work it out.

Chapter Twenty-Nine: Terminal Triumph

May I have the envelope, please?

And the winner for best actor is—

Eddie Longo for "Terminal Triumph"!

CLAP CLAP CLAP CLAP

I wanna thank the Academy, and everyone connected to the making of "Terminal Triumph"—

But more than anyone else, I want to express my special thanks to the woman most responsible for me being up here—

My former wife and my best friend, Mae Longo!

Mae, honey. I know you're listening, and I know you're as thrilled as I am. And I just wanna say that the second I get off this stage, I'm on my way to your house

to share this award with you, because it's your as much as mine!

See ya in a minute, pal!

CLAP CLAP CLAP CLAP CLAP CLAP CLAP CLAP

Ricky, the rest of you guys wait here. I want this to be a special moment.
Then, in five minutes, Ricky, you bring in the photographers.
Mae!
Look who's here, honey!

Chapter Thirty: Wrap Party

Remember my story? I had a story.
A beginning, a middle, and an end.
I told my story, I sang it, I meant it,
It was my only story,
And now I repent it.
All that I knew, I thought it was true,
I don't know anymore what I think,
And do you?
What is your story, is it truer than mine?
Will you speak plainly,
Or will you give it a shine?
Invent your own story,
I'm done telling mine.
Lady Veil's

Acknowledgments

Victor Giannini typed the first draft and googled photos of thirties cars, street scenes, interiors, and what all.

Tula Holmes typed revisions, ruled and erased pages, googled thirties and forties fashions, World War II uniforms, cars, planes, more what all.

Zelie Rellim typed the final draft, erased pages, googled jungle scenes, forties armaments, hospital interiors, Hollywood exteriors and interiors, even more what all.

Turner Classic Movies, plus a 65-inch Blu-ray high-definition flat screen, and the pause button on my remote, so that I could re-create the look of noir. No problem. It posed for me.